THE ADVENTURES OF
Brer Rabbit
and Friends

This book belongs to

from Dorling Kindersley

*The Family Learning mission
is to support the concept of
the home as a center of
learning and to help families
develop independent learning
skills to last a lifetime.*

Project Editor Natascha Biebow
Project Art Editor Lisa Lanzarini
Senior Editor Marie Greenwood
Managing Art Editor Jacquie Gulliver
Picture Researcher Louise Thomas
DTP Designers Kim Browne & Jill Bunyan
Production Joanne Rooke

Published by Family Learning
Southland Executive Park
7800 Southland Boulevard
Orlando, Florida 32809

Dorling Kindersley registered offices:
9 Henrietta Street, Covent Garden, London WC2E 8PS
www.dk.com

Published in Great Britain by Dorling Kindersley Limited.

Library of Congress Cataloging-in-Publication Data

Amin, Karima, 1947—
The adventures of Brer Rabbit and friends : from the stories collected by Joel Chandler Harris /
retold by Karima Amin ; illustrated by Eric Copeland. — 1st American ed.
p.   cm.
Summary: A retelling of the classic African American tales about Brer Rabbit and his friends and enemies,
animals who are constantly on the prowl to fool each other.
ISBN 0-7894-4925-0
1. Afro-Americans Folklore.   2. Tales—United States.   [1. Afro-Americans Folklore.   2. Animals Folklore.
3. Folklore—United States.]   I. Harris, Joel Chandler; 1848–1908.   II. Copeland, Eric, 1938— ill.   III. Title.
PZ8.1.A49 Ad 1999   398.24′52′08996073—dc21   99-14241   CIP

Color reproduction by Bright Arts, Hong Kong
Printed and bound by L. Rex, China

Acknowledgments:

The publisher would like to thank the following for their kind permission to reproduce the photographs:

t = top, b = bottom, a = above, c = center, l = left, r = right.

Bruce Coleman Ltd.: Erwin and Peggy Bauer 63tr, Robert P. Carr 62br, Stephen J. Krasemann 62cl(below), Steven C. Kaufman 63c; **Corbis UK
Ltd.:** Library of Congress 60tl, U.S Army Military History Institute 60bl; **Mary Evans Picture Library:** 60/61bc; **Little, Brown and Company:**
From SUNGURA AND LEOPARD by Barbara Knutson. Copyright © 1993 by Barbara Knutson. By Permission of Little, Brown and Company
61tr; **N.H.P.A.:** John Shaw 62bc, 62c(below), 63cr, Stephen Krasemann 63tl; **Oxford Scientific Films:** Breck Kent / Animals Animals 2cl(above);
Oxford University Press: Illustrated by Joan Kiddell-Monroe taken from *African Myths and Legends* © 1962, by permission of Oxford University
Press 61c; **Planet Earth Pictures:** Brian Kenney 63br, Ken Lucas-Photo 63bc; **Still Pictures:** Jorgen Schytte 61tl; Special Collections Department,
Robert W. Woodruff Library, Emory University 60tr. **Jacket: Corbis UK Ltd:** Library of Congress back flap.

The publisher would particularly like to thank the following people: Lodina Clyburn and "Youth for a Better Tomorrow,"
Epiphany Church, Buffalo, NY; Tom Hicks, Wildlife Division, Georgia Department of Natural Resources;
Carole Mumford, The Wren's Nest House Museum, Atlanta, GA; Ian Campbell, Jane Thomas & Claire Watson;
Cathy Tincknell & John Woodcock (additional illustration); Tanya Tween (jacket artwork border); David and Lynn Bennett.

THE ADVENTURES OF
Brer Rabbit and Friends

From the stories collected by JOEL CHANDLER HARRIS

Retold by **Karima Amin**
Illustrated by **Eric Copeland**

FAMILY LEARNING

Contents

From the Storyteller

I WAS A LITTLE GIRL when I first met Brer Rabbit; my mother brought him into our house and into my life. I still remember how the stories she told used to make me laugh until my stomach ached and my eyes watered. How I loved it when my uncle James drew for me "that ole rabbit kickin' up the dust" – Brer Rabbit hurrying off to the next adventure.

Many years later, I learned that Brer Rabbit was a hero/trickster character created by my foreparents, enslaved Africans who endured a cruel, harsh life on plantations in the southern states of America. Brer Rabbit first came to life in print in 1878, when a journalist named Joel Chandler Harris wrote down a few of the stories for a Georgia newspaper, *The Atlanta Constitution*. He recorded the stories *exactly* as he had heard them told by African-Americans he had met. The stories were so well-liked that Harris collected enough to fill eight volumes. These are now recognized as the largest single collection of African-American folktales ever published.

Reading the original Harris tales is no easy task for modern readers. In this book, I have retold ten stories in easy-to-read language for readers to enjoy again. I have kept familiar words and expressions traditionally used by African-Americans, such as "Brer," short for "brother," an affectionate term used by our people to express family feelings. And because Brer Rabbit's origins are so interesting and important, this book includes background information about the stories. I know you'll like my friend Brer Rabbit – he's funny and smart and a lot like you.

Karima Amin

Brer Rabbit's World

THE STORIES IN THIS BOOK have been told for many, many generations. They are part of the traditions of African peoples who were forced into slavery and brought to the southern United States to work on plantations in the 18th and 19th centuries. These people lost their freedom, but they brought with them their memories and their stories. As time went by, the stories began to include the animals and places these enslaved Africans saw around them on the plantation. That's how Brer Rabbit and his friends came to be.

Plantation owners lived in big houses.

Main house

Kitchen

Dairy

Storehouse

Vegetable garden

Many plantations grew their own food.

Food stayed cold and fresh in the springhouse.

Shed

Slave quarters

Slave homes were small and cramped.

Creek

Stables

Chicken coops

Livestock was kept for meat and dairy products.

The stream provided drinking water.

Brer Fox
When he's not chasing up Brer Rabbit for dinner, Brer Fox is sure to be scheming in his fencerow den.

Brer Weasel
Wily Brer Weasel lives in fencerows, too. He can easily fool his friends by playing on their weak spots.

Brer Turkey Buzzard
Brer Buzzard acts as judge for the animals from his perch in the trees.

Brer 'Coon
Brer 'Coon loves to run around, so he's not often at his home by the swamp.

Woods

Slaves worked
all day tending
crops in the
hot sun.

Cotton field

Fencerows are areas of
vegetation that grow
along fences or walls.

Wheat was ground in
the mill to make flour.

Mill

Briar patch

Mill pond

Swamp

Orchard

Grasses

Match the characters'
footprints with those
on the map to find out
where they might live.

Brer Rabbit
Sassy Brer Rabbit
gets a thrill out of
outsmarting the
other animals
on the plantation. He lives
in the briar patch.

Brer Bear
Brer Bear lives
with Mrs. Bear
and the twins
in the woods.
Here, plenty
of honey and
berries keep their
furry bellies full.

Brer Possum
Brer Possum is
at home in the
hollow of a tree.
But more often
than not he's
out and about being too
curious for his own good.

Brer Wolf
Brer Rabbit
should beware
of Brer Wolf
stalking through
the woods. His
hungry chops
are always after
rabbit for his stew.

**Miz Meadows
and the Gals**
The herons enjoy a good
gossip whenever Brer
Rabbit comes a-courtin'
them in the swamp.

**Brer
Snake**
In the tall, wild
grass of his home,
slimy Brer Snake can
sneak up on the other
animals in no time.

Brer Terrapin
Brer Terrapin lives with
his family in some
brambly bushes.
He's not as
slow as Brer
Rabbit thinks.

Brer Mink
Shy Brer Mink makes
his home by the
stream; when night
falls, he sneaks
out to hunt fish
and birds.

How Brer Rabbit Lost His Fine Bushy Tail

HAVE YOU EVER taken a good look at a rabbit from behind? Then you know that ol' rabbit's got a bob-tail. That's right! Thanks to Brer Rabbit, he's got a bob-tail! Now, way back in the beginning, things were different; Brer Rabbit used to have a long, bushy tail. Let me tell you how he lost it.

Brer Rabbit's fine tail was his pride and joy. In the cool of the evening, he'd take his stroll down the big road just to show it off, strutting his stuff with a "lippity-clip, lippity-clip" and a "howdy-do?", waving that tail to all the folks as he passed.

Swishy-swish... swishy-swish...

Every now and then, for added measure, he'd give that fancy tail a shake and a twirl. The gals liked that and he knew it. That long, fine, bushy tail was the talk of the town. Some folks had great admiration for it, while others were a bit jealous. That was one pretty tail!

Swishy-swish...
swishy-swish...

One evening, Brer Rabbit
was going down the road, waving,
shaking, and twirling his tail, when he saw
Brer Fox ambling along with a big string of
fish. They spent a moment or two passing the time
of day, then Brer Rabbit asked, "Brer Fox, tell me,
whereabouts did you find that nice string o' fish?"
"I caught these down at the creek," said Brer Fox.

"Those minnows you have there are the kind I like. How did you catch 'em?" Brer Rabbit asked.

Brer Fox said, "It was simple. I went to the creek after sundown, dropped my tail in the water, and sat there 'til daylight. With my tail, I caught a whole armful of fish. I had so many that I flung some back into the creek!"

Now you and I know that don't sound right but Brer Rabbit wasn't thinking about the right or wrong of it. He was already tasting minnows.

Later that evening, Brer Rabbit found himself a spot on a log where he could squat and drop his tail into the creek. The weather was cold that night so he had brought along something warm to drink. He sat there, and he sat there, just a-squattin' and a-drinkin' 'til by 'n' by the sun came up.

Brer Rabbit stood up to check his catch, but his tail was stuck in the frozen creekwater. He pulled and pulled, then groaned and pulled again. Then he heard: "R-r-r-r-rip!" Brer Rabbit looked around. His tail was gone!

Now, I don't know if Brer Fox was jealous or not, or if he tricked Brer Rabbit on purpose. Maybe he just gave Brer Rabbit some bad advice. But I do know this: from that day on, all Brer Rabbit's kin had short tails just like him.

Brer Fox and Brer Rabbit Go Hunting

I**N SPITE OF ALL** that you may have heard or read, there were times when Brer Rabbit and Brer Fox were friendly with one another. They would sit together and sip their drinks and play a game of checkers or horseshoes, and chew the fat like no hard feelings had ever rested between them. But Brer Rabbit never forgot how Brer Fox caused him to lose his tail.

One day, Brer Fox came along all dressed up and asked Brer Rabbit to go hunting. "Howdy, Brer Rabbit! I'm goin' huntin' today, and I'd be much obliged for your company," he called.

"G'mornin', Sir. Thanks for the invitation, but I've got other fish to fry," Brer Rabbit replied with a wink.

"Well I'm sorry you can't join me," said Brer Fox. "Have a nice day."

Brer Rabbit winked again. "I always do."

Brer Fox set off to hunt, and Brer Rabbit found himself a nice spot for a nap.

Brer Fox was gone all day, and had a mighty, powerful streak of good luck. His game bag was heavy and just about full as he headed home.

H-m-m-m-m...

Brer Rabbit had napped, on and off, all day long. Toward evening, he got up, scratched himself, stretched, and said, "H-m-m-m-m . . . It's almost time for Brer Fox to be gettin' home. I wonder if I can see him comin'."

Brer Rabbit
hopped up onto a
tree stump and looked
into the distance for Brer
Fox. Soon, there he was,
coming through the woods,
singing like a rooster at sunrise.

Brer Rabbit leaped off the stump, then took off his clothes and
hid them in the bushes. He rolled in the dust, then lay in the road
like he was dead.

Brer Fox came along and examined him. "Look at this fat,
dead rabbit. He's the fattest rabbit I ever did see. Looks like he's
been dead a long time." Not a peep came out of Brer Rabbit.

Brer Fox licked his chops. He turned Brer Rabbit over and said,
"Maybe he's been dead for *too* long. I'm afraid to take him home."
So he went on his way, leaving Brer Rabbit lying in the road.

When Brer Fox was out of sight, Brer Rabbit jumped up,
grabbed his clothes, and dashed off through the woods to get ahead
of Brer Fox. Once again, he hid his clothes and rolled in the dust.

When Brer Fox came up, there he found Brer Rabbit, looking cold and stiff. "Look-a-here, look-a-here – another fat, dead rabbit!" he exclaimed. "Where are they all comin' from?"

Brer Fox studied on this for a while then unslung his game bag. "These rabbits are going to waste," he said. "I'll leave my bag here and go back to get that other rabbit. When folks see me with a bag full o'birds and animals, including two fat rabbits, they'll be thinkin' that I'm old man Hunter from Huntersville. Ha-ha-ha!"

Ha-ha-ha! Ha-ha-ha!

Brer Rabbit opened one eye to watch Brer Fox lope up the big road to the spot where he had left the first rabbit. When Brer Fox was nowhere to be seen, Brer Rabbit hopped up, dressed himself, and ran off with Brer Fox's game bag.

Lippity-clippety, lippity-clippety.

When Brer Rabbit saw Brer Fox next, he called out, "Hey! What d'you catch the other day, Brer Fox?" Looking somewhat embarrassed, Brer Fox hollered back, "I caught a handful of common sense, Brer Rabbit."

"Hee-hee-hee!" Brer Rabbit laughed. "If I had known that's what you were hunting, I'd have loaned you some of mine."

Brer Rabbit and the Tar-Baby

YOU KNOW, Brer Fox tried more than once to catch Brer Rabbit.
Once he came mighty close to doin' it with somethin' he made
called a Tar-Baby.

One day, Brer Fox mixed up some tar and turpentine, and then
he molded it into the shape of a baby. He put a hat on it and sat it
in the big road, right where Brer Rabbit was known to stroll every
morning. Brer Fox eased off to hide in a ditch where he could watch
the happenin's.

By 'n' by, Brer Rabbit came along just struttin' his stuff with a

Lippity-clippety, lippity-clippety.

When he saw the Tar-Baby, he pulled up on his hind legs and
looked astonished.

"Good mornin'!" said Brer Rabbit.

Tar-Baby just sat there and Brer Fox, low in the ditch, winked.

"Sure is nice weather!" said Brer Rabbit.

Tar-Baby didn't say nothin' and Brer
Fox, low in the ditch,
smiled big.

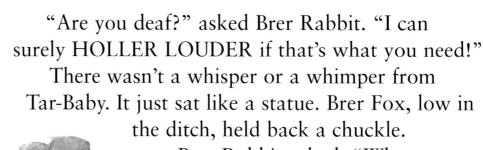

"Are you deaf?" asked Brer Rabbit. "I can surely HOLLER LOUDER if that's what you need!" There wasn't a whisper or a whimper from Tar-Baby. It just sat like a statue. Brer Fox, low in the ditch, held back a chuckle.

Brer Rabbit asked, "Why you so stuck up? Can't you tip yo' hat and say 'Howdy' like you got some manners? I don't know what yo' problem is but I bet I can fix it!"

Tar-Baby's lips didn't move. Brer Fox's eyes got a glint. Brer Rabbit drew back with a fist, then whacked Tar-Baby on the side of the head. WHACK! Brer Rabbit's fist stuck fast.

"If you don't turn me loose," shouted Brer Rabbit, "I'll whack you again!"

Tar-Baby sat still, and Brer Fox lay low. WHACK! Now *both* Brer Rabbit's fists were stuck in the tar and he squalled, "Turn me loose now, or I'll give you a kick like you ain't never had befo'."

Tar-Baby still didn't move an inch.

By now Brer Rabbit was hopping mad. He kicked both feet then butted his head into the tar.

THUNK! THUNK!

WHOP!

Then Brer Fox sauntered out of the ditch with, "Howdy, Brer Rabbit! You lookin' kind of stuck up this morning!" Then he rolled on the ground and laughed, "I've got you now, you bob-tailed rascal! Now you know who's boss. I've had enough of you mindin' other folks' business. Who asked you to get friendly with Tar-Baby? Look at yo' self, all stuck up. Looks like you 'bout to be my barbeque dinner."

It was a mighty humble sounding Brer Rabbit who said, "I guess you've got me now. Actually, I'm pleased to be barbequed. It's a whole lot better than being thrown into the briar patch."

"On second thought," said Brer Fox, "it's too much trouble to make a fire so I'm going to hang you."

"Go on and hang me! Hang me as high as you like, but please don't toss me into that briar patch!" pleaded Brer Rabbit.

"Looks like I ain't got no string or rope so I expect you'll be drowning this morning," threatened Brer Fox.

"Yes, drown me! Drown me! Please drown me. I don't care so long as you don't fling me into the briar patch," begged Brer Rabbit.

"Hm-m-m-m . . . looks like there ain't no water nearby so I'll have to skin you," replied Brer Fox.

"Thank you for the skinning, Brer Fox. You can snatch out my eyeballs, rip my fur and my ears out by the roots, and cut off my legs but, please, please, please don't throw me into the briar patch," pleaded Brer Rabbit.

Now you know Brer Fox wanted to hurt Brer Rabbit real bad so he grabbed him by the ears, pulled off the Tar-Baby, swung him around overhead, then flung him into the briar patch. There was a little commotion when Brer Rabbit struck the bushes, then silence.

Brer Fox waited for a moment until he heard, "Yoo-hoo!" Lookin' off yonder, he saw sassy Brer Rabbit as happy as can be, chuckling to himself in the briar patch.

Brer Rabbit waved. "Hey, Brer Fox!" he cried. "I was born and raised in the briar patch. The briar patch is my home!" Then off he skipped with a

Lippity-clippety, lippity-clippety.

Brer Fox learned that day that the biggest folks don't necessarily have the biggest brains. Little folks, born and raised in the briar patch, can be mighty smart.

Brer Rabbit's Riding Horse

B RER RABBIT stayed close
to home for a few days
after getting mixed up with
the Tar-Baby. It took him
a while to get all the
tar out of his fur,
but he did it.
Some folks
didn't expect
him to make
a quick
and sassy
comeback,
but he did that too.

Ol' Brer Rabbit came back just as sassy, if not sassier, than before.

When Brer Rabbit paid Miz Meadows and the gals a visit
a few weeks later, they laughed and teased him about getting all
stuck to the Tar-Baby. Sitting on the porch with him, the ladies
went on and on with a monstrous gigglement.

Brer Rabbit just sat there listening, cool as a cucumber. By and
by, he crossed his legs, gave a little grin and a slow wink, and said,
"Ladies, Brer Fox was my daddy's ridin' horse for thirty years,
maybe more, but thirty years for sure."

He dropped that line just like that, tipped his hat, and called,
"Good day, ladies!"

Hip-hop, hip-hop he strutted, like a man with a plan.

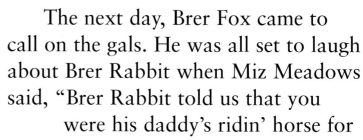

The next day, Brer Fox came to call on the gals. He was all set to laugh about Brer Rabbit when Miz Meadows said, "Brer Rabbit told us that you were his daddy's ridin' horse for thirty years."

Brer Fox got hot but he didn't say a word.

Miz Meadows and the gals twittered and chattered on. Brer Fox still didn't say a thing until he rose to leave.

"Ladies, I ain't disputin' what you say, but I'll make Brer Rabbit eat his words and spit 'em out, right here where you can see 'em."

With that, he left to make a straight shoot to Brer Rabbit's house. Brer Rabbit was expecting him; he had his door shut tight.

Brer Fox knocked on the door. Nobody answered. He knocked again. Still no answer. When he knocked a third time –

BLAMITY BLAM! BAM BAM BAM! –

Brer Rabbit called out in a weak voice:

"Is that you, Brer Fox? I want you to run and fetch the doctor. I ate a little bit of parsley this mornin' and it's done made me sick. Please, Brer Fox. I need the doctor."

Brer Fox said, "I'm here to fetch you. Miz Meadows is havin' a party and all the gals are there. They said it wouldn't be a real party without you, so here I am to bring you along."

Brer Rabbit moaned, "I'm mighty sick."

"No you ain't!" Brer Fox barked.

"I'm too sick to walk so far," complained Brer Rabbit.

"No problem," said Brer Fox. "I'll tote you in my arms."

"Oh, no," whined Brer Rabbit. "You might drop me."

"Well, then I'll tote you on my back."

Brer Rabbit considered that and said, "That sounds pretty good, but I'll be needing a saddle to help me sit steady and a bridle to hold on to."

"Well . . . I don't . . ." stammered Brer Fox.

BLAMITY BLAM! BAM!

Brer Rabbit continued, "I'll be needing a blind bridle so that you don't shy at stumps along the road and fling me off. You know I really don't feel well, but a party might be exactly what I need to make me better."

Brer Fox said, "Okay. I'll let you ride me almost to Miz Meadows' door, then you can get down and walk the rest of the way."

While Brer Fox ran off to get the saddle and blind bridle, Brer Rabbit whistled gaily, getting ready for the party. He combed his fur and greased his whiskers.

Soon, Brer Fox trotted up to the door, looking like a circus pony, wearing a saddle and blind bridle. He even pawed at the ground and chomped at the bit like a horse.

Brer Rabbit mounted Brer Fox and they took off for the party.

Trot trot. Trottety, trot trot trot.

With the blind bridle on, Brer Fox couldn't see behind him. So when he felt Brer Rabbit raise one of his feet, he asked, "Hey, what you doin'?"

"I'm just shortening the left stirrup," Brer Rabbit said.

By 'n' by, Brer Fox felt Brer Rabbit lift his other foot.

"What you doin' now?" Brer Fox asked.

"Fixin' my pants," Brer Rabbit replied.

All along, that wily rabbit was puttin' on a pair of sharp spurs. When they got close to the spot where Brer Rabbit was supposed to get off and walk, Brer Fox stopped and Brer Rabbit jabbed those spurs into Brer Fox's flanks.

OOOWWWWW!

howled Brer Fox, and took off faster than greased lightning.

Buckity-buck. Buckity, Buckity-buck.

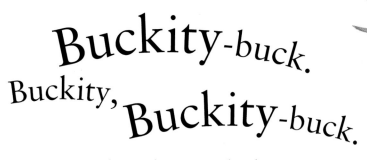

When they reached Miz Meadows' house, the gals were sitting on the porch. They watched in amazement as Brer Rabbit rode by at top speed. Way down the road they saw him come to a halt and turn his "horse." Then he came trotting back, stopped, and hitched Brer Fox to the horse rack at the front of the house.

He sauntered up the steps to the porch, tipped his hat and took a seat. "Ladies," he said, "didn't I tell you that Brer Fox was our ridin' horse? His gait ain't what it used to be, but he's still got a few good years left."

Brer Rabbit grinned. The gals giggled. Miz Meadows said, "Brer Rabbit, you sure do have a fine pony."

Hitched to the rack, poor ol' Brer Fox thought of a thousand ways to trick a rabbit and wondered which one would take care of Brer Rabbit for good.

A Mighty, Big Noise in the Woods

Early one fall morning, Brer Rabbit was stirring around in the woods looking for a sweet-scented plant called bergamot. Miz Meadows and the gals loved the way it made his hair look and smell. The wind blew kind of cold that day but Brer Rabbit was determined to keep his reputation as a fine-looking, sweet-smelling fellow. As he searched about, hoppity-skippity, lippity-clippity, he heard someone off in the distance cutting down a tree. Brer Rabbit listened. The saw whirred and whirred until by-and-by the tree came down – KLUBBER-LANG-**BANG**-**BAM!** That mighty, big noise made Brer Rabbit jump a mighty, big jump and he took off.

Now, Brer Rabbit wasn't scared, he was just taking care of himself.

He ran, and he ran, and he ran until he was just about out of breath. About then, he ran into Brer 'Coon.

"Yo, Brer Rabbit!" hollered Brer 'Coon. "What's your hurry?"

"Got no time to tarry!" wheezed Brer Rabbit.

"Folks sick?" asked Brer 'Coon.

"No, thank goodness. Got no time to tarry!"

"Well, what's the matter?" demanded Brer 'Coon.

"Mighty, big noise back there in the woods. Got no time to tarry!" panted Brer Rabbit.

This made Brer 'Coon feel kind of nervous, especially since he was far from home. He took off, a-boiling through the woods and ran straight into Brer Fox.

"Hey, Brer 'Coon, where you going?" asked Brer Fox.

"Got no time to tarry!" wheezed Brer 'Coon.

"Going for the doctor?"

"No, Sir! Got no time to tarry!" answered Brer 'Coon.

"Tell me the news, Brer 'Coon, good or bad!"

"Oh . . . there's a mighty, queer racket back there in the woods! Got no time to tarry!"

Without a moment's
hesitation, Brer Fox leaped up and fairly
split the wind with his running, until he met Brer Wolf.

"Hey you, Brer Fox! Stop and rest yourself," said Brer Wolf.

"Got no time to tarry, Brer Wolf!" hollered Brer Fox.

"Who needs the doctor?" asked Brer Wolf.

"Not a soul! Got no time to tarry!" wheezed Brer Fox.

"Please tell me, Brer Fox! What's happenin'?"

"There's a mighty, strange fuss back there in the woods.
Got no time to tarry!" cried Brer Fox.

When he heard this, Brer Wolf nearly scorched the earth,
taking off from that place. He ran and he ran until he met
Brer Bear.

Brer Bear asked the question and Brer Wolf made the
answer: "There was a terrifying commotion back there
in the woods."

At that, Brer Bear ran off, as fast as he could.

Soon, all the critters were running, all because of that "mighty, big noise back there in the woods."

Bakatak, bakatak. Kirik, kirik. BaDambang, BaDambang. Lop, lop!

By 'n' by, they all ended up at Brer Terrapin's house.
Brer Terrapin asked, "What's all the excitement?"
"A terrifying commotion . . . !" Brer Bear growled.
"A mighty, strange fuss . . . !" Brer Wolf howled.
"A queer racket . . . !" Brer Fox barked.
"There was a mighty, big noise back there in the woods!" Brer 'Coon added. "The fact is, we've got no time to tarry!"

Brer Terrapin asked, "What did it sound like?"
Each critter answered, "Uh . . . I don't know . . . Can't say for sure . . ."

Brer Terrapin asked, "Who heard the mighty, big noise?"
Each critter answered, "I didn't . . . Nope, not me . . ."

Brer Terrapin chuckled. "Now, if you all are still feeling a bit skittish, then run along. I'm gonna stay right here and cook my breakfast. But, if I hear any kind of strange noises, I just might follow along behind you."

The critters looked at one another then started to make inquiries amongst themselves. Eventually it seemed that all the news about the "mighty, big noise" could be traced back to Brer Rabbit, who wasn't even there! The critters decided to set out for Brer Rabbit's house.

They found him sitting on the front porch, enjoying the sun.

Brer Bear spoke first: "Why d'you fool me, Brer Rabbit?"

"Fool who, Brer Bear?"

"Fool me, Brer Rabbit. That's who!"

"Hold on, Brer Bear! I ain't seen you all day, 'til now."

All the critters asked the same question: "Why d'you fool me, Brer Rabbit?" They all got the same answer until Brer 'Coon spoke up:

"Well, you surely did see *me* today, Brer Rabbit! Why did you make a fool out of me?"

"How did I do that?" asked Brer Rabbit.

"You pretended that there was some queer racket in the woods."

"Brer 'Coon, there was a racket – a mighty, big noise in the woods."

"What kind of noise?" asked Brer 'Coon.

"I suspect you should have asked me that first, Brer 'Coon."

"I'm asking NOW!"

"Someone cut down a tree in the woods. If you had asked me, I would have told you," smirked Brer Rabbit.

Feeling kind of silly, all the critters moseyed off with Brer Rabbit's words ringing in their ears. Brer Rabbit smiled a big, contented smile, and leaned back in the sun.

Brer Rabbit Finds His Match

I KNOW YOU'RE PROBABLY saying to yourself, "That Brer Rabbit was a mighty smart fellow," and you're right. But every now and then, just when he was beginning to get a little too big for his britches, some critter would come along and take the wind right out of his sails. Brer Terrapin did just that. He made Brer Rabbit sit up and take notice.

One fine day, Brer Rabbit and Brer Terrapin were discussing this and that and that and this when they got to disputing who was faster. Brer Rabbit bragged and boasted, long and loud, about his amazing speed. However, Brer Terrapin was not to be outdone. With a warning in his voice, he said, "Alright now, Brer Rabbit. You'd best not be starting what you can't finish. A fifty dollar bill in a chink in my chimney back home says I can outrun you."

With a smug little smile, Brer Rabbit said, "I've got a fifty dollar bill too, and my money says that *I'll* be fifty dollars richer at the end of the race."

Brer Rabbit and Brer Terrapin agreed to race on the next day.

Miz Meadows and the gals and all the critters, far and near, were invited to the great race.

Brer Turkey Buzzard was chosen to be the judge and the stakeholder. He and his crew marked off the distance of a five-mile run around the plantation with mileposts set up along the way.

On the day of the race, Brer Rabbit was to run down the big road. Brer Terrapin said he'd run through the woods near the big road. Folks told him that didn't seem wise, but Brer Terrapin had a plan.

Brer Rabbit prepared at home in his yard by limbering up with a lippity-clip, and a skippity-skip.

Brer Terrapin prepared down in the swamp by holding a family meeting with his wife and their three children.

Now everybody in Brer Terrapin's family was the spitting image of him. Even if you had a spyglass and took a good look at them, you wouldn't know one from the other.

Early in the morning, on the day of the race, each of the Terrapins took their place, off in the woods, near a different milepost. Mrs. Terrapin waited at the first one; the Terrapin kids took up their positions at the next three mileposts, followed by Brer Terrapin at the last one.

By 'n' by, Miz Meadows and the gals and all the critters assembled to see how the race would come out. Brer Rabbit arrived with ribbons streaming from his ears. Judge Turkey Buzzard, looking mighty important, strutted around with a watch.

At last, Judge Turkey Buzzard hollered, "Gents, you ready?"

Brer Rabbit and *Mrs.* Terrapin (in the woods) hollered back, "Yes!"

Judge Turkey Buzzard gave the signal, "Go!" then flew overhead to keep an eye on things.

Brer Rabbit took off with a

lippity-clip, and a skippity-skip.

When he reached the first milepost, he called out, "Where are you, Brer Terrapin?"

"Here I come skedaddling," said Mrs. Terrapin, as she crawled out of the woods toward the first milepost. Brer Rabbit took off again, while Mrs. Terrapin put out for home.

At the second milepost, Brer Rabbit hollered out again, "Where are you, Brer Terrapin?"

"Here I come a-boiling fast," said Brer Terrapin's daughter, Lilly Terrapin, as she crawled toward the second milepost.

Brer Rabbit lit out again, while Lilly Terrapin made her way home.

When a still confident Brer Rabbit reached the third milepost, he saw Brer Terrapin's son, Billy Terrapin, who shouted, "Here I come a-crawling strong."

Brer Rabbit kept on a-movin' with a lippity-clip and Billy Terrapin went on home.

At the fourth milepost, Brer Terrapin's other son, Terry Terrapin, waved at Brer Rabbit and hollered, "What happened? Did you get lost?"

A surprised Brer Rabbit didn't answer. He just thought to himself as he moved on, "I guess Brer Terrapin isn't such a slow coach after all." Terry Terrapin scrambled on home.

Brer Terrapin looked up and saw Judge Turkey Buzzard skimming along, so he knew Brer Rabbit must be close to finishing the race. He shuffled out of the woods, through the crowd of folks, then stood behind the winning milepost.

By 'n' by, here comes Brer Rabbit, ribbons draggin' . . . pushin' hard . . .

clip-clip . . . clip-clip . . . clip-clip,

to the finish line. To Judge Turkey Buzzard he wheezed, "Gimme the money. Gimme the money."

Just then, Miz Meadows and the gals and all the critters began to hoot and holler with laughter as Brer Terrapin stepped out to say, "As soon as I catch my breath, I believe *I'll* be fingerin' that money!"

Brer Rabbit was fit to be tied as Brer Terrapin, with a purse full of money tied around his neck, slow-walked his way home.

Life is funny. Just when you think *you're* the smartest, someone smarter comes along.

Brer Rabbit's Astonishing Prank

BRER RABBIT was a genuine prankster. No one was better at pulling off a prank than Brer Rabbit. Even when the other critters just happened to get the better of him, no one could bounce back like Brer Rabbit. He was, without a doubt, the smartest, the funniest, and the luckiest critter around.

One time, ol' Brer Rabbit decided to pay a call on Brer Bear. When he got there, he saw the Bear family leaving the house.

Brer Rabbit stood in the woods by the side of the road considering, "Since Brer Bear and I are more mad with each other than friendly right now, perhaps I'd better wait a minute and visit *after* they're gone."

So he waited until the Bear family were out of sight, then slipped into the house and began having a ransacking good time. He was peekin' and pokin' and openin' and

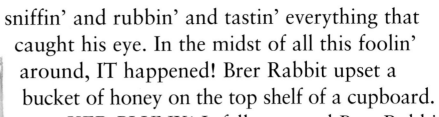

sniffin' and rubbin' and tastin' everything that caught his eye. In the midst of all this foolin' around, IT happened! Brer Rabbit upset a bucket of honey on the top shelf of a cupboard.

KER-PLUNK! It fell over and Brer Rabbit got covered with honey from head to toe.

It was much more than a few drips and a couple of dollops. Brer Rabbit had honey *everywhere*, including his eyeballs!

Wiping the honey out of his eyes, Brer Rabbit moaned, "What am I gon' do? I'm in a mess o'trouble. If I go outside, the horseflies and the bumblebees will get me. If I stay here, Brer Bear will catch me for sure."

It didn't take Brer Rabbit long to figure out which would be worse. He waddled outside, and tried to clean himself off with dry leaves. He rolled on the ground, this way and that way, but it only made his situation worse – now Brer Rabbit was covered in leaves *and* honey!

He tried to shiver-shake the leaves off:

a-shake-a-shake-a-shaky.

But the leaves didn't budge. He tried to jump 'em off:

Hippity-hop . . . Hippity-hop.

But that didn't work either.

Brer Rabbit tried shaking and jumping and wiggling and spinning around, and who knows what else, but nothing got the job done. He was one big, noisy, honey-leaf mess.

So Brer Rabbit decided to put out for home.

Swishy-swushy, splishy-splushy.

Strolling on the big road toward home, Brer Rabbit met up with Sis Cow. She took one look at the "honey-leaf thing" that was Brer Rabbit, raised her tail, and ran like dogs were after her.

Brer Rabbit laughed big, and strolled on with a

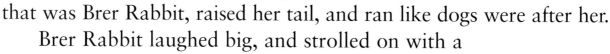

swishy-swushy, splishy-splushy.

Next he saw a little girl taking some pigs to market. When they caught sight of the "honey-leaf thing," they took off, running fast and squealing loud.

Brer Rabbit laughed even bigger and kept on going.

Swishy-swushy, splishy-splushy.

He went on like that for a while, scaring everybody he met. Each time his laughing (and his head!) got bigger and bigger. Soon Brer Rabbit got to wondering what it would be like to scare Brer Fox. While he was considering this, something made him stop laughing.

Coming up the road was Brer Bear and his family. They stopped and took a good look at the "honey-leaf thing."

The "honey-leaf thing" looked at the bears, then walked straight up to them. It gave itself a hard shake, then jumped straight up in the air.

Mrs. Bear howled, dropped her parasol, and climbed a tree. The twins skedaddled through the bushes, and Brer Bear tossed the picnic basket into the air and made a fast break through the woods.

Brer Rabbit laughed. "I'm a tough man!" he boasted feeling mighty biggity.

On he strutted, until by 'n' by, he saw Brer Fox and Brer Wolf.

They had their heads together, plotting ways to catch Brer Rabbit. While this plan and that plan had their full attention, they didn't even notice the "honey-leaf thing" until it was right in front of them. They stepped aside to give "it" plenty of room on the road.

Now Brer Wolf wanted to show off in front of Brer Fox so he played big by asking Brer Rabbit who he was.

Brer Rabbit jumped up and down in the middle of the road and hollered:

I'm Big Boy Dan,
and I'm a HUNGRY man,
and you're the one I'm after!

Taking another big jump, Brer Rabbit pretended to take off after Brer Fox and Brer Wolf. Without blinking, Brer Fox and Brer Wolf lit out from there faster than greased lightning!

For a long time after that, whenever Brer Rabbit saw Brer Fox and Brer Wolf, he'd hide behind a bush or a stump and holler out:

I'm Big Boy Dan,
and I'm a HUNGRY man,
and you're the ones I'm after!

Brer Fox and Brer Wolf would break and run every time, and Brer Rabbit would laugh hard enough to bust a gut.

Brer Rabbit Catches Wily Brer Weasel

SOME CRITTERS don't like to admit it, even today, but there were times when they had to call Brer Rabbit to help them solve their problems. Once, when they all lived and worked together and kept their butter cool in the springhouse, the critters noticed that there was some butter-snitching going on. Every day some butter would be missing.

Brer Mink, Brer Possum, Brer Wolf, and the others started hiding the butter in different places inside the springhouse to fool the thief, but that didn't work. Eventually they discovered the butter-snitcher's tracks. It was wily Brer Weasel!

All the folks had a meeting and decided to take turns standing guard over the butter. They agreed that anyone who failed to catch the thief would lose the right to eat butter for one year.

Brer Mink sat up with the butter first. His eyes and ears were pretty sharp, so he watched and listened and waited until he got cramps in his legs. About that time, Brer Weasel popped his head in the door.

"Hey, Brer Mink! I've been lookin' for you. Come on out with your lonesome-lookin' self and play hide-and-go-seek with me."

Brer Mink thought to himself, "If Brer Weasel is playing, he can't steal the butter. Right? Right!"

So Brer Mink played with Brer Weasel until Brer Mink was so tired, he sat down to rest and fell asleep.

This was Brer Weasel's chance to steal the butter, and you know he did. When the theft was discovered, Brer Mink's name was marked down on a list and his butter-eating days were through.

Next it was Brer Possum's turn to stand guard. By 'n' by, Brer Weasel came in with a, "Howdy, Brer Possum!"

Brer Possum sat still and said, "Keep movin'."

Tickle tickle tickle

Knowing that Brer Possum was kind of ticklish, Brer Weasel started tickling him in the short ribs. Brer Possum laughed and Brer Weasel tickled him some more. Then, while Brer Possum lay on the floor laughing and panting for air, Brer Weasel took as much butter as he wanted. Brer Possum's name joined Brer Mink's on that list of those whose butter-eatin' days were done.

Brer 'Coon was next to stand guard.

He hadn't waited long before that wily Brer Weasel sidled up and challenged him to a race.

"Ready! Set! GO!" cried Brer Weasel, and off they went. They ran and ran until Brer 'Coon just had to stop and rest. And while he rested, Brer Weasel shot right back to the springhouse and nibbled butter until he was content.

No more butter for Brer 'Coon, either.

Puff puff puff!

Squawk!

Next to watch the butter was Brer Fox. He was mighty confident because he knew that Brer Weasel was afraid of him. Brer Weasel *was* afraid, but that didn't stop him. He studied on it for a while then figured out a plan to handle the situation.

Somehow, Brer Weasel managed to coax some chickens from a nearby coop up to the springhouse. When Brer Fox saw those fine, fat hens, he didn't waste no time runnin' out to grab a few. While he enjoyed a hearty chicken dinner, Brer Weasel enjoyed that sweet springhouse butter.

Brer Wolf was the next watcher. Brer Weasel was afraid of him too, so he stood off a ways from the springhouse, disguised his voice, and called out, "Look at these nice, tender lambs. I sure do wish Brer Wolf could see 'em."

When Brer Wolf heard that, he didn't waste a minute before loping off after those tender lambs.

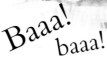

Baaa! baaa!

Squawk!
Squawk!

And while Brer Wolf was off chasing his dinner, Brer Weasel skipped into the springhouse and helped himself to some of that delicious creamy butter for *his* dinner.

The names of Brer Fox and Brer Wolf joined the others whose butter-lickin' days were done.

Brer Bear, guard number six, was sitting near the springhouse door when Brer Weasel walked in. "Howdy, Brer Bear! I just stopped by to see if you needed me to take any fleas or ticks off your back."

"Howdy, yo'self and thank you," Brer Bear replied.

With that, Brer Weasel began to rub and stroke Brer Bear's back and scratch his sides. Brer Bear liked that; he felt good and relaxed. It didn't take him long to fall asleep and lose *his* butter-eating privileges, too.

Those poor critters didn't know what to do about Brer Weasel. They discussed their problem for a long time before admitting that they needed Brer Rabbit to get them out of this mess.

Hmmm...

At first, Brer Rabbit wasn't convinced. He thought they were conjurin' up some trick to catch him. Finally he agreed to watch their butter. With a long piece of string in his pocket, Brer Rabbit hid in the springhouse where he could keep a close eye on the butter.

Here comes Brer Weasel creepin' in and lookin' all around. He didn't see anybody so he went for the butter.

"Let the butter alone!" hollered Brer Rabbit.

Brer Weasel stopped cold. "That you, Brer Rabbit?"

"The one and only. Now go on 'way from here."

"But the butter's sooo . . . sweet! Please let me get just one little taste," Brer Weasel begged.

"Let it be!" Brer Rabbit ordered.

Changing his tune, Brer Weasel crooned, "Sure is a nice day for a footrace . . ."

"I'm tired," Brer Rabbit grumbled.

"I surely do love to play hide-and-go-seek," Brer Weasel continued.

"Been there. Done that," Brer Rabbit muttered.

The two of them kept it going back and forth until Brer Rabbit suggested a new game. Taking that long piece of string out of his pocket he said,

"Let's play tug-o'-war. Let's tie our tails to this piece of string. Then we'll pull to see who is stronger."

Brer Weasel agreed, so they tied each other's tails to the ends of Brer Rabbit's string. Brer Weasel stayed inside the springhouse while Brer Rabbit went outside. Once outside, Brer Rabbit untied the string from his tail and tied it around a tree.

"PULL!" he shouted.

Brer Weasel tugged and strained and pulled for a long time then called out, "It's a draw! Looks like we've got equal strength. Come and untie me!"

Brer Rabbit just smiled.

"Come on, UNTIE ME!" yelled Brer Weasel.

But Brer Rabbit didn't pay that weasel no mind. He just settled down to wait on a log outside. When the critters came to check on their butter, they found Brer Weasel all tied up inside the springhouse. They had nothing but great appreciation for Brer Rabbit, who, they had to admit, was much smarter than they were.

Brer Possum and Brer Snake

You should've seen Brer Possum that day. The smile on his face was as big and bright as the big, yellow sun above his head as he thought aloud, "My, my, my . . . what a beautiful day! My, my, my . . . what a wonderful world!"

Then a surprised Brer Possum muttered, "My, my, my . . . what is this big, ol' hole doin' here in the middle of the road?"

At first Brer Possum considered, "I think I'll just walk on around this hole and go on 'bout my business." But he didn't do it.

Then he thought, "I reckon I'll just walk on around and go on back home."

But he didn't do that either, 'cause he was curious. So he walked over to the hole and he took a little peek inside. There was Brer Snake, lying long and fat in the cool mud at the bottom.

Brer Snake had a smile on his face, too, but it wasn't big and bright like Brer Possum's. His was kind of sneaky looking. There he lay in the mud, looking up at Brer Possum. When Brer Possum saw that snake, he took off running up the road –

bookity, bookity, bookity–

exclaiming, "I don't want nothing to do with snakes!"

But he hadn't gone far when he heard a little voice calling, "S-S-s-S-s-save me, Brer Possum! Come and he-e-elp me!"

Now you and I know what Brer Possum should have done. He should have kept on running –

bookity, bookity, bookity–

up the road for home, but he didn't do it. He sauntered back to the hole trying to look and sound rough and tough. "Hey you, Brer Snake! What do you want from me?"

Brer Snake looked up and his voice was syrupy sweet when he pleaded, "I'm S-s-S-stuck in this hole and I need your help. Please take this brick off my back and help me get out."

"Not a chance!" said rough and tough Brer Possum. "I won't help you. You are a snake and you'll bite me for sure."

Brer Snake's voice was as sweet as the spring water on a hot summer's day when he replied, "But I n-e-e-ed you . . ."

"Well, let me think it over," said Brer Possum. After thinking and pacing up and down, and back and forth, and all around, he noticed a dead tree branch and he had a brilliant idea.

Sticking that branch into the hole, he used it to push the brick off the snake's back. Easing that branch under Brer Snake's belly, he lifted him out of the hole, then tossed him into the tall grass.

"Whew!" exclaimed Brer Possum with a mixture of relief and pride. "He didn't bite me! I'm pretty smart!"

Then he took off running –

bookity, bookity –

up the road. But he hadn't gone far when he heard, "S-s-s-s-save me, Brer Possum! Come and he-e-elp me!" Now you and I know what Brer Possum should have done. He should have kept on running –

bookity, bookity, bookity –

up the road for home, but he didn't do it. Trying to look rougher and tougher, Brer Possum walked back to the hole.

"I'm getting mighty tired of that snake

wasting my time," he grumbled.

But when he noticed that the tall grass was everywhere, and he realized that Brer Snake could be hiding anywhere, that angry look quickly disappeared and a scared look took its place. "Uh . . . Brer Snake . . . where are you? Come on now . . . Brer Snake . . . where are you?"

After a minute or two, Brer Snake came wiggling and squiggling out of the tall grass. In a voice as sweet as candied yams and as smooth as buttermilk, he murmured, "Brer Possum, I'm "S-S-s-s-o cold. I was wondering if you wouldn't mind putting me in your pocket so I can get warm."

"You want to bite me, don't you?" asked an accusing Brer Possum.

"Who me? I'm just cold and I . . ."

"Are you going to bite me?" Brer Possum asked point blank.

"But I n-e-e-e-ed you . . ." the snake whis-S-s-spered.

Brer Possum took a long look at Brer Snake and thought, "He sure does look sad. Looks cold, too . . ." Then reluctantly he mumbled, "Okay . . . One time in my pocket should be alright."

So Brer Snake coiled up to become possum-pocket size, and Brer Possum scooped him up and put him inside his pocket.

The snake was so quiet and so still that Brer Possum forgot all about him until he heard: "S-S-s-s! I'm going to bite you."

Brer Possum stammered, "Uh-uh-uh . . . . why would you do that? I took the brick off your back and got you out of that hole. What's more, I let you rest in my nice warm pocket. What's goin' on?!"

Brer Snake sneered, "You knew I was a S-S-snake when you put me in your pocket."

Brer Possum sighed. "Since I'm going to die, please let me go down to Brer Rabbit's house and tell him good-bye."

"Alright. Be quick about it," Brer Snake snapped.

Brer Possum found Brer Rabbit on his front porch. "Good mornin', Brer Rabbit!" he called.

"Howdy do, Brer Possum! Where are you goin'?"

"Where am I going? I'm going to die. I've got a snake in my pocket."

"My goodness, what're you doin' with such a dangerous critter in your pocket?" exclaimed Brer Rabbit.

Brer Possum told Brer Rabbit about meeting the snake. When he finished, Brer Rabbit said, "That's quite a story! Hey, Brer Snake! What d'you say?"

Brer Snake stuck his head out of Brer Possum's pocket and said, "Yup, that's what happened."

Brer Rabbit looked kind of puzzled and said, "Well I can't understand it. Let's go down to where the thing happened. I think that'll help to make the picture clear."

So they all went to the hole together.

"Now where were you at the start?" asked Brer Rabbit.

"I was here in this hole," said Brer Snake, crawling back to his place in the mud next to the brick.

"Well, I was going home, minding my own business," explained Brer Possum, "when that evil rascal sad-mouthed me here to this spot where I'm standing now. Now, this here is the branch I used to push the brick off his back," continued Brer Possum, handing the branch to Brer Rabbit.

Quick as a flash, Brer Rabbit shouted, "Gotcha!" and pushed that brick back onto Brer Snake's back.

Thanks to Brer Rabbit, Brer Possum learned a good lesson: don't go looking for trouble, because you just might find it.

The Moon in the Mill Pond

ONE EVENING Brer Rabbit ran up on ol' Brer Terrapin. "I'm just itchin' to have me some fun," said Brer Rabbit.

Brer Terrapin grinned and replied, "Then you're the very one I've been lookin' for."

"Well then," said Brer Rabbit, "it's about time we put Brer Fox, Brer Wolf, and Brer Bear on notice. Let's have us a little fishin' frolic down by the mill pond tomorrow night. I'll do the talkin' and you can just sit there and back me up by agreein' with everything I say."

Brer Terrapin laughed. "If I ain't there, then you know a grasshopper done flew away with me."

You could almost see Brer Rabbit's mind working on the plan. "Let's put out the word that we're gonna have us a grand ol' time. Let's say, 'We'll be partyin' and fishin' all night long!'"

Brer Terrapin grinned some more and drawled, "I hear ya, Brer Rabbit."

Then Brer Rabbit winked at Brer Terrapin and whispered, "Now, don't you go bringin' yo' fiddle 'cause there really won't be no need."

With a knowing nod, Brer Terrapin drawled again, "I hear ya, Brer Rabbit."

With that, Brer Rabbit put out for home and went to bed. Brer Terrapin set out for the mill pond so he could be there on time.

The next day, word about the fishin' frolic went out to all the critters. They thought it surely did sound like some fun.

That night, Brer Wolf and Brer Bear came with a hook and line. Brer Fox came with a dip net and Brer Terrapin brought the bait. Miz Meadows and the gals brought themselves and found a comfortable spot away from the edge of the pond.

Brer Fox said, "I'm goin' for perch this evenin'."

Brer Wolf said, "I'm lookin' to catch some hornyheads."

Brer Bear said, "I'm tryin' for catfish tonight."

Brer Terrapin said, "I'm out to catch some minnows."

Brer Rabbit winked at Brer Terrapin and said, "I'll be fishin' for suckers."

Then Brer Rabbit marched up to the pond, acted like he was about to cast his line, and stopped cold. All the folks turned to watch him. He leaned forward and stared at the water. Folks began to get uneasy, especially Miz Meadows, who twittered, "My goodness, Brer Rabbit! What is it? What's the matter? Is it a snake?"

In a hushed voice, Brer Rabbit mumbled, "I don't believe it . . ."

For a long while, Brer Rabbit didn't say a word. He just kept looking and scratching his head. By and by, he sighed deeply and said sadly, "Well, ladies and gentlemen, it looks like this here fishin' frolic is over. We may as well pack up our gear and go."

Brer Terrapin ambled over to the edge of the pond and looked in. He slowly shook his head and said, "I hear ya, Brer Rabbit . . ."

Brer Rabbit said, "Don't be scared, folks. We got us a little problem here. Accidents do happen; the Moon done fell into the water. If you don't believe me, look for yourself."

They all crowded along the bank, looked in, and saw the Moon swingin' and swayin' at the bottom of the pond.

Brer Fox said, "Well, well, well."

Brer Wolf said, "Mighty bad, mighty bad."

Brer Bear said, "Mmmmh, mmmh, mmmh."

Miz Meadows and the gals said, "Tsk, tsk, tsk. Now, ain't that too much?"

In a no-nonsense voice, Brer Rabbit said, "Until we get the Moon out of the pond, there'll be no fishin' here."

Brer Terrapin piped up with, "That's right, that's right."

"Well, how we gonna get the Moon out?" the others asked.

Brer Terrapin replied, "Uhhh . . . we'd better leave that to Brer Rabbit."

Brer Rabbit made a big show of rolling his eyes, scratchin' his head, and pacin' back and forth. Then he said, "If I can borrow Brer Mud Turtle's big seine net, we can drag the Moon out. What d'ya think, Brer Terrapin?"

Brer Terrapin agreed. "Sounds good to me. I'm sure you'll find my Uncle Mud willing to help us out."

Brer Rabbit went to borrow the net. While he was gone, Brer Terrapin told the folks all the stories he had heard all his life that said: "He who fetches the Moon out of the water, will also fetch out a pot of money."

When Brer Fox, Brer Wolf, and Brer Bear heard that, they agreed that since Brer Rabbit was so kind as to go after the net, they would do the hauling.

When Brer Rabbit returned, Brer Terrapin winked at him and it didn't take Brer Rabbit long to figure out what was going on. He pretended that he really wanted to go in after the Moon. He quickly took off his suspenders and was just about to shuck his shirt when Brer Fox, Brer Wolf, and Brer Bear insisted that it just wasn't right for a fine gentleman like Brer Rabbit to go into the water. After protesting (just a little), Brer Rabbit handed over the net to them.

Brer Fox and Brer Wolf each grabbed an end. Brer Bear, dragging behind, caught the middle, so that he could unsnag the seine net if it got caught on a log.

They made one haul – no Moon. They hauled a second time – no Moon. Stepping out further, where the water was getting mighty deep, they hauled again and shook their heads to get the water out of their ears. While they were shaking, they lost their footing and fell into the pond. SPLISH! SPLOSH! SPLASH! Down and up, they kicked, sputtered, and sloshed!

When they came out, coughing and dripping, Miz Meadows and the gals snickered and Brer Terrapin laughed and laughed.

Brer Rabbit took a quick peek at the Moon high in the sky and hollered, "I guess you gentlemen had better go on home and get into some dry clothes." He sniggered. "Perhaps we'll have better luck next time! You know, they say the Moon will only bite at a hook if you use fools for bait!"

Sheepishly, Brer Fox, Brer Wolf, and Brer Bear sloshed out of the pond and went off home, dripping, through the woods.

Under the warm glow of the Moon in the sky, Brer Terrapin and Brer Rabbit slow-walked Miz Meadows and the gals back home, laughing and sniggering all the way.

Tales from Africa

Uncle Remus

T HE BRER RABBIT STORIES were first collected and published by American journalist Joel Chandler Harris in 1878. As a young man, Harris trained as a printer's apprentice on a plantation in Georgia. He liked to visit the slaves in their cabins and listen to the Brer Rabbit stories that had been handed down for generations. Years later, Harris wrote down these stories for others to enjoy, too. He created a fictional narrator called Uncle Remus, based on several slaves he had met.

Joel Chandler Harris (1848–1908)

Life on the plantation

Plantation owners forced enslaved Africans to work all day. Some tended crops, such as sugar cane, tobacco, and cotton. Others worked in the main house. Slaves had a hard life with no rights. Sharing traditional stories and songs helped them keep up their spirits. Freedom finally came in 1865, after the American Civil War.

The overseer's job was to keep order in the fields.

Small slave cabins often housed several families under one roof. It was in a cabin much like this that Harris first heard the Brer Rabbit stories.

Sungura and Leopard

AFRICAN TRICKSTERS

In many East African stories, the trickster is a rabbit, too. Sometimes he is called Zomo or Sungura; his rivals include Elephant, Lion, and Leopard – animals that are native to Africa – rather than Fox or Wolf as in the Brer Rabbit stories.

Anansi tricks Lion.

Storyteller wisdom

The stories in this book originally came from Africa, where the storyteller is an important part of the community. Storytellers pass on traditional values and history. They often tell stories about people they know, but disguise them as animal characters so no one's feelings will be hurt.

ANANSI, THE SPIDER MAN

The main trickster in West African stories is Anansi, the Spider Man. Like Brer Rabbit, Anansi can outsmart almost any other animal – except Land Turtle. Anansi sometimes appears as a man, but when he is in danger, he changes into a spider.

Children as young as ten were forced to work in the fields.

Storytellers, like the author, help to keep traditional tales alive.

Tell us a story

All over the world, children and adults enjoy animal trickster tales about Brer Rabbit, Sungura, and Anansi. People tell stories to share their cultures, their beliefs, and their histories – stories that teach and entertain.

Meet the Animals

THE ANIMALS in this book were all once
native to the southern United States
where the Brer Rabbit stories are set.
As cities grew and plantation fields were replaced by woods for timber
production, the animals were pushed out of their natural homes. This,
along with pollution and hunting, means that some animals are now rare.

Brer Terrapin

Terrapins, like this painted box turtle, have very long lives. They live both

in water and on land, and feed on wild
berries, slugs, earthworms, and mushrooms.

Brer Rabbit

The rabbit in the Brer
Rabbit stories is the eastern
cottontail rabbit. It hides from
his enemies – foxes, owls,
coyotes, and people – in
the briar patch.

Rabbits come out
at dusk to feed
on grasses.

Brer Mink

Minks live near water.
They come out at night to
stalk their prey – ducks, mice,
crabs, and fish. Minks were
once trapped by people for
their fur and are now
endangered.

Miz Meadows and the Gals

Blue herons live in
swamps and coastal
areas. These tall,
graceful birds feed
on a rich diet of
fish and frogs.

Brer 'Coon

Raccoons have nimble
fingers that can easily pry
off the lids of garbage
cans in the middle of
the night. They also
eat fish, crayfish,
berries, and seeds.

You know,
if you're ever looking for
some fun, just
go find Brer Rabbit.
Some folks say
"FUN"
is his middle name.

Brer Bear

Sharp claws help black bears climb trees to escape danger from other bears and people. Black bear cub Bears hibernate in the winter; during the rest of the year, they roam large areas to find carrion (dead animals), fish, ants, acorns, berries, grubs, and honey for food.

Brer Weasel

A weasel on the lookout

Although small, weasels are fearless hunters. They prey on moles, shrews, rabbits, and rodents. Their enemies include foxes, snakes, owls, and hawks.

Brer Turkey Buzzard

Turkey Buzzards have a keen sense of smell that helps them track down dead animals for food. They also eat small animals and other birds' eggs.

Brer Wolf

A rare red wolf

Wolves hunt in packs and cover great distances each day to catch rabbits, deer, and rodents for supper. They have a taste for sheep, so many have been shot by farmers. This has made them an endangered species.

Brer Fox

Foxes eat almost anything – rabbits, lizards, rats, berries, birds' eggs, and even scorpions, complete with stingers. They live in fencerows and fields. The fox in the Brer Rabbit stories, called the gray fox, can climb trees very quickly.

Brer Possum

Strangely enough, possums, or opossums, sometimes eat snakes! They also eat insects, birds' eggs, fruits, and nuts. When threatened by enemies such as foxes or coyotes, possums play dead. Mother possums carry their young in a special pouch.

A scarlet kingsnake

Brer Snake

There are thousands of different types of snakes. Some eat mammals, such as possums; others feed on birds, insects, and other reptiles' eggs.